Fiery Attraction

Emma Richmond

Harlequin Books

TORONTO • NEW YORK • LONDON
AMSTERDAM • PARIS • SYDNEY • HAMBURG
STOCKHOLM • ATHENS • TOKYO • MILAN
MADRID • WARSAW • BUDAPEST • AUCKLAND

Special thanks and acknowledgment to Emma Richmond

ISBN 0-373-15297-3

FIERY ATTRACTION

First North American Edition 1995.

This edition Copyright © 1995 by Harlequin Enterprises B.V.

Copyright © 1993 by Emma Richmond.

Printed in U.S.A.

One

Just one more day, she reassured herself as she absently filed a ragged nail. And then, Domini, you need never see him again. Three days of constant dictation, typing, trying to catch up on a backlog of work, because the last temp had been useless, because he didn't trust any of the other secretaries in the company—and now there was a lull—momentary, she was sure—in which to catch her breath. Normally she would have taken it all in her stride, but because he was the sort of man she disliked most she found it difficult to relax. He was arrogant, capable, assured—and a womaniser. Not that she *cared* what he did in his private life—she just found it incomprehensible that a man of his ability should waste his private life so—frivolously. A man she could have admired. Creative, imaginative. A brilliant entrepreneur.

The door slammed open, and the subject of her thoughts strode in.

He walked across to the desk, looked down at the closely written pages of the report he had given her the previous evening, glanced at the blank computer screen, and back to Domini. "You've forgotten how it works?" He was also odiously sarcastic.

"No."

"You couldn't read my writing?"

"I could."

"But you have a ragged nail."

"Yes," she agreed. Picking up the papers he'd just been looking at, she handed them to him. "You will, presumably, want these back. And these," she added softly. Picking up the transcript she had stayed late the previous evening to finish, she held it out.

His expression unchanged, he took it. "Games?"

"No. I never play games—as you very well know."

"So I do. Bring your book through."

As soon as she was seated in front of his massive desk, he sat in his swivel chair, swung his feet up, and steepled his fingers under his chin.

They watched each other. Like hawk and eagle, she thought and, being objective, he was gorgeous, in a casual sort of way. Eyes of that very pale, almost colourless blue, startling with their dark lashes. He was tall and slim; his thick, dark hair was shaggy, over-long, and he had a habit of shoving it back off his forehead. The face was intense, with high cheekbones, and a wide mouth. A very determined chin.

He looked like a gunslinger—and she had absolutely no desire to play Cowboys and Indians.

"Letter to Henderson Graphics—you'll find the address in the file. Is everyone here?"

"Yes, all in the boardroom, waiting," she added.

"Let them wait." And he began to dictate, smoothly, clearly, with an economy of words that she would, in different circumstances, have appreciated enormously. He knew what he wanted to say, and said it in a voice that was dark, deep, full of sexual promise. Unconscious? Or deliberate? And when he'd finished dictating he went back to staring at her with maddening insolence. "And I still find it extremely difficult," he drawled, "to equate the way you look with the way you act."

"Try harder," she encouraged sweetly.

"And I did wonder," he continued, "when you first walked through my door, whether the almost ecstatic praise I received when I made enquiries was for other than your secretarial skills."

"I know."

"I don't give up easily," he warned.

"Neither do I. Go into your meeting, Mr. Wellby, you've kept them all waiting long enough." Rising, she picked up her papers.

"Sensuous and earthy. Volupt—"

"Don't," she warned. "Just don't."

He gave a wicked grin. "Nicely rounded? Generous?"

Refusing to be provoked, she pushed through the connecting door to her office. "Generous figure" she would accept—from anyone but him—but *not* "voluptuous"! And sensuous and earthy? As far as she knew, she had never been either in all of her twenty-nine years. But why on earth couldn't the gods have made her coolly sophisticated instead of looking like a—sex pot? And just *why* did people equate efficiency only with stick-thin, haughty-looking girls? It was extremely unfair.

The meeting finally broke up at gone three. Jack returned to his office and firmly closed the door. But when there had been no communication by four-thirty, and knowing he'd wanted his letters to go that night, Domini tapped on his door, and walked quietly through. He stared at her, his face irritated.

"Letters?" she prompted.

With an impatient sigh, he unclipped his pen. "I assume I don't need to read them?"

"No," she agreed. "They're quite correct."

"Yes. Why do I even bother to ask?"

Standing beside him, she noted the way his hair brushed his collar, the healthy shine, then gave herself an impatient shake. There was nothing about this man that interested her—nothing.

"Send some flowers to a Miss Jane Gower, will you?"

With a little start, she exclaimed, "What?"

"Day-dreaming, Miss Keane? Not like you."

"No. Flowers?"

"Yes, *not* red roses. Thirty-seven Pelby Street."

"Message?"

"Mmm. Thank you, Jack."

"Thank you? For what? Services rendered?"

"No need to sneer, Miss Keane. What I do in my private life is no concern of yours."

"How true." Picking up the last letter, she walked away. On Monday, there had been flowers for a Marguerite Edwards. He *was* a busy little boy, wasn't he?

No sooner had she reached her desk than the buzzer sounded.

"Get Grogan up here."

"Now?"

"Yes, Miss Keane, now! And then you can go. I shan't need you any more tonight."

Thank goodness. And what had poor Grogan been up to? When he arrived she warned kindly, "If you've any misdemeanours on your conscience, think up a good excuse now, because he is on the war-path."

"Oh, hell. Thanks, Domini." Taking a deep breath, he tapped firmly on Jack's door and went in.

She couldn't hear what was said, only a low rumble of voices as she put on her coat, then went thankfully downstairs and out into the fresh air.

Walking along to London Bridge, she mentally shook off her business image, allowed a small smile to grow. She loved London, loved the busyness of it, liked to watch the faces—and if she could finish papering the hall ceiling tonight, well, that would leave the weekend free. And soon, it would be spring, and she could get busy in her little walled garden.

Friday morning, Jack strode in, halted opposite her desk, and stared at her. "Decided to stay?"

Ah, back to friendly mockery. "No," she denied.

"Think of the money."

"Think of the damage to my reputation," she returned.

"But you're the best—the *crème de la crème*—and you deserve to work for the best. Me."

"Oh, yes, impatient, irritable, sarcastic..."

"Domineering, charismatic, decisive," he put in. "And you really shouldn't believe everything you read in the Press," he reproved. "Just because my picture is often—"

"Don't you have any work to do?" Domini interrupted, refusing to be charmed by him. Then the phone rang. "Just a moment, please." Her face devoid of expression, she purred, "Marguerite for you."

His smile was very wry. "Such perfect timing that woman has. Put it through, will you?" He walked into his own office.

He made several telephone calls, and when he eventually called her through he was standing at the window, staring down into the street, hands in his pockets. His jacket was over the back of his chair, and the light-hearted mood had gone.

"Right, memo to all departments." It was scathing, proclaiming that if they didn't get their collective fingers out there would be no company for them to be employed in.

"When you've typed that, bring me in the files of all customers, past and current, and a list of future orders. Oh, and Doug Lever is coming in this afternoon, so see we're not disturbed."

"And I'm sorry for the foul mood," he tacked on. "Nothing to do with you. In fact, if they were all as efficient as you there wouldn't be a problem."

When Doug arrived, she collected him from Reception.

At just after four she heard both men leave. When neither had returned by five, she cleared up, made sure everything was as she'd found it five days before, and then quietly left. Walking towards the station, she felt vaguely dissatisfied, and didn't really know why. Because she hadn't been thanked? That was daft. She didn't want to work for Jack, although when he wasn't being impossible he was actually quite nice... Irritated by her preoccupation with this man, she hurried up the station approach. And yet she *had* enjoyed the challenge of working for him.

"And where the devil do you think you're going?" Jack demanded from close behind her.

With a startled squeal, she spun round.

"Sorry," he apologised, "but I need to talk to you."

"We have nothing to talk about."

"Yes, we do. Stop being difficult."

"Mr. Wellby," she insisted, "we have nothing to say. Now I really must go or I'll miss my train."

"I'll drive you," he said.

"I don't *want* you to drive me! And will you please let go of my arm?"

"No, and I'm damned if I'm going to hold this discussion in the street." He began tugging her back the way she'd come.

"My car's just over here."

"I don't care where it is! And will you please stop tugging me along the pavement? I do not want you to take me home!"

"Why?"

"Because..." Because I don't want you to, you stupid man. Taking a deep breath, Domini was then frustrated by the appearance of a traffic warden officiously opening her notebook, and then taken by surprise when Jack tugged open the door of his Bentley and shoved her inside. "That's better," he exclaimed.

"It is not! And will you please let me out of this car?"

"No, not until you agree to hear me out."

"Oh, good grief," she sighed. She had no desire for him to take her home—the only alternative was to tell him she'd changed her mind, or to listen to his wretched proposals. "All right, all right," she agreed. "Stop the car. I'll listen."

"I can't stop it here, Domini," he reproved, "so I might just as well take you the rest of the way."

"Very well," she agreed icily. "You'd better take the next left. Mr. Wellby! This is *not* the way to Greenwich!"

"I know."

"But you said you were taking me home."

"I am—my home."

Oh, no. Alarm bells jangling horribly, she began, "Mr. Wellby—"

"It was Jack just now."

"No, it wasn't, but—" Taking a deep breath, she asked really quite calmly, "Where exactly is your home?"

"Surrey."

Surrey. Right, good; that wasn't so far, and her brother Nick was at Surrey University, so in an emergency...

"And why do we need to go to Surrey to talk?" she asked in the same desperately calm tone.

"Because I promised the children that I wouldn't be late," he explained with all the sweet reason of a snake.

Children? What children? His? He was *married*? Glancing at him sideways, she glanced just as quickly away. He was smiling, and that, for some reason, made her even more angry.

"For someone who wanted to have a discussion," she snapped, "you're being remarkably reticent!"

"I don't like to talk while I'm driving," he said smoothly. "And no need to look so agitated, you'll be adequately chaperoned."

"Good." Who by? His wife and children?

"When I got back to the office and found you gone, I was furious! I'd left a message with that dratted receptionist that I'd be late back and to ask you to wait."

"Well, I didn't get the message," she told him flatly.

"Obviously, otherwise you would have got to the station before I could catch up with you. Wouldn't you?"

"Yes," she agreed defiantly. Turning to face him, she exclaimed despairingly, "I don't *want* to work for you."

He gave a faint smile, then encouraged, "Come on, Domini, don't cut off your nose to spite your face. You're the best secretary I've ever had. And very decorative," he added. He sounded as though he had his tongue very firmly in his cheek.

"There are other equally efficient secretaries," she muttered.

"I dare say there are."

"Then why me?" she burst out.

"I don't know," he admitted softly. "Because of your obvious antipathy, which intrigues me?"

"Oh, don't be absurd."

"Is it? Why do you dislike me so much, Domini?"

"I don't," she denied stiffly. "Only your..." Breaking off, deciding that it would be stupid to get into personalities, she changed it to, "I only like doing temporary work."

"Then work for me temporarily. Six months?"

"No."

"Three?"

"No."

"One? How about it? The agency isn't doing too well at the moment, is it? No, don't fire up. I wasn't trying to blackmail you. But it isn't, is it?"

"No," she said reluctantly.

"And I would be fully prepared to pay agency rates and not try to poach you."

"You couldn't."

"No, because you are very loyal to your friend there, aren't you? So will you at least think about it?"

The agency did need the money. So did she, if she was ever to get her roof mended and finish everything that needed doing in her little house.

"I give you my word that I will never chase you round the desk," he persuaded with presumably the same tongue position as before. "I meant what I said, Domini. An efficient secretary is what I want, nothing more. I'm neither a fool, nor, despite your conviction, a Don Juan, and I take my business very seriously.''

Yes, of course he did; that was why he was so successful. And it was rather arrogant to assume that he would—pester her. Chewing indecisively on her lower lip, she leaned back in her seat and tried to formulate rational arguments for and against becoming his secretary.

TWO

With a sigh, wondering why she was even *considering* his proposal, she watched curiously as he turned into the driveway of his house. Detached, warm red brick, square. A no-nonsense sort of house, which she would have said, from his impressive track record in the business world, suited him to a T.

His housekeeper didn't look much older than Domini herself, and she gave Jack a suspicious glance.

"Her husband also works for me," he told her blandly. "Diddy, this is Miss Keane, who might become my secretary."

"Might?" She smiled.

"Mmm. Make us some tea, would you?"

"Yes of cour— Oh, that wretched phone hasn't stopped ringing all day!" Picking up the hall phone, she listened, then said, "New York."

"Oh, right, thanks. I'll take it in my study. Look after Miss Keane for a minute, will you?"

Diddy smiled. "Come on through to the lounge and I'll make that tea. Don't mind children, do you?"

"No," Domini said, but wasn't entirely sure that she wanted to meet Jack's children. Walking into the room the housekeeper indicated, she smiled as two pairs of eyes turned to survey her, the little girl's with suspicion, the little boy's with apparent delight. The little girl was about eight, thin as a rail, plain as a pudding, her dark hair scragged back. She got to her feet and turned the TV set off. The little boy, blond, four or five years old, also got up, a beaming smile on his face. "Hello," she said, grinning. "I'm Domini."

"Hello," the little girl said solemnly. "I'm Amelia, and this is Angus. We've been out to tea," she announced.

"Well, you both certainly look very smart."

"Yes." Turning only her head, the little girl looked her brother up and down as though checking that he still looked as he was supposed to. "I got him ready."

Domini dutifully inspected him. Then, still smiling at the children, she encouraged, "Don't let me stop you watching the television . . ."

"They shouldn't be watching it anyway," Jack said from behind her. "Or Angus shouldn't, should he?" he asked. "I do believe it's way past his bedtime."

"He was waiting to say goodnight to you," Amelia said.

"Then I had best do so," Jack agreed, scooping up the little boy. "Goodnight, monster. Sleep tight—don't let the bedbugs bite."

Angus giggled, gave Jack a resounding kiss, then leaned across to give Domini one. A little nonplussed, she kissed him back, avoiding the wicked gleam in Jack's eye, and smiled lamely at Amelia, who smiled back. "He likes kissing ladies," she explained.

Well, she knew where he got *that* from!

"Ready?" Jack asked as he put the boy down.

With a little nod, Domini moved to the door that he was holding open, and as she passed he whispered softly, "I can see you're going to be a real asset."

"Meaning?" she asked lightly.

"Meaning, should I ever need a baby-sitter..."

"Wrong," she denied. "If I'd wanted to be a nanny, I would have trained as one." And then she asked, "Yours?"

"My what?"

"Children!"

"Good God, no!" he exclaimed. "They're my niece and nephew. They're here temporarily, while my brother's house is being renovated."

"Oh—well, it's none of my business . . ."

"True . . ."

"So I think we had better get back to the business in hand," she insisted firmly, making herself comfortable in one of the study's squashy leather armchairs.

He perched on the edge of his desk, looked amused, then thoughtful. "Some of this you will already know, but bear with me. I am, I suppose, an investor. Films, plays, businesses. If I think it will make money, I invest."

"And Hargreaves Office Furniture was one of the businesses you invested in."

"Mmm, the banks refused to lend them any more money, and because I thought they were worth saving, I did so. And up until recently, everything was going well. They should have retained their profitability."

"But didn't."

"No. Complacency, Miss Keane. However, with Doug Lever newly appointed to the helm, hopefully they'll be back on the road to recovery. Now, I already know that you are efficient, have all the necessary office skills, but do you also work as well unsupervised?"

"Yes."

"No need to be offended—if I don't ask, I don't get told, do I? So, in brief, most of the time—if you agree to work for me," he tacked on, "you will be in charge of the office and will sometimes need to make your own decisions, because I won't always be able to be reached. I have a stockbroker, of course, and a lawyer, and they will advise if there is ever any difficulty— and I will not hold you responsible for any errors of judgement. What I will hold you responsible for is stupidity, or failure to act at all. The hours will sometimes be long, but you can take time off, if it is justified, and I shall not demand explanations, providing," he added pointedly, "that I know where you can be reached."

"That sounds as if you expect me to be on call at all times."

"I do. Whenever I need you, I'll call. Including evenings and weekends."

"And you'll expect me to abandon whatever I'm doing and come running?"

"Yes. I shall be paying you well enough to ensure that you do just that. It probably won't be often, but I don't conduct all my business during office hours. Occasionally I'll need you with me in order to dictate a report while it's fresh in my mind." He added, "And some of those meetings will be abroad. You have a current passport?"

"Yes."

"Keep it up to date. Ditto your driving licence."

It sounded—interesting. Don't lie, Domini—it sounded terrific—if only she could get over this feeling of danger. She continued to stare at him, not really seeing him, but seeing the near future.

"Salary paid monthly into your bank account, agency fee paid separately. Yes or no?"

Yes or no? "It *will* be a strictly professional relationship?" she stressed quietly.

"It will."

"Mmm." Knowing she would be a fool to turn it down, she made up her mind. "Yes, all right. But on a one-month trial basis," she qualified.

"Fair enough. Questions?"

"Not at the moment. I will have later, I expect."

"OK." Pulling a pad towards him, he quickly scribbled something, tore the sheet off, and handed it to her. "Address of the office. I'll meet you there at ten o'clock Tuesday morning. I still have some things to clear up at Hargreaves on Monday. Yes?"

"Fine."

"Good. Don't change your mind, will you?"

"No," she denied, still with a slight feeling of reluctance, of having been rushed.

On Tuesday morning, Domini walked along Philpot Lane to Jack Wellby's office. There was no name-plate outside, no obvious number—for security reasons? Because he didn't want uninvited callers? She could only suppose so. Pushing open the outer door, she walked up the funny little staircase to the first floor, and tapped on the door.

The man who answered it was of medium height, slim, with sandy hair. "Miss Keane?"

"Yes," she smiled.

"Right. Well, better come in, then. I'm Jeff."

Sumptuous was her first impression. Thick carpet, highly polished old furniture, crammed bookshelves. One massive desk by the window—presumably Jack's—a wide archway, through which she walked, and two more desks. One on the right, obviously hers, the other in the far corner, presumably Jeff's.

"Er—Mr. Wellby's been held up," he mumbled.

"Mr. Wellby's already here," his deep voice pronounced from behind them. "Good morning, Miss Keane. Morning, Jeff." He sounded amused.

He also *looked* amused, and Domini raised one eyebrow in query. "You find something funny, Mr. Wellby?"

"Yes. I walked behind you up Philpot Lane. And some poor chap was so busy turning to watch you that he walked into a lamp-post."

"And that's *funny*?"

"Well, I thought so. Here," he held out a key. "You'll be needing this to get in and out. Don't lose it."

She took it and walked across to her desk.

"Small wash-room to your left, keys to the filing-cabinets in top right-hand drawer," he explained. "Anything else you need to know, ask Jeff."

By the end of the first day, her wariness had gone, because, true to his word, never by look or deed did Jack try to create any intimacy between them. He was polite, friendly, slightly formal. She called him Mr. Wellby; he called her Miss Keane. Which was fine, wasn't it? And so it continued for the next few weeks.

He stretched her in ways she had never been stretched before, believed her capable of things she had no idea she was capable of. She spoke with film stars and producers. MPs and million-aires, and after the initial excitement, she be-came blasé about it all. And now there was a lull, and Domini was able to catch up on a report Jack had asked her to read. Just as she'd got in-volved in it, the door opened and a beautiful blonde walked in. How? Because she hadn't latched the door properly. Oh, knickers!

"Can I help you?" Domini asked.

"Are you Domini?" she asked throatily.

"Yes," Domini admitted cautiously.

"Oh, good. I'm Marguerite. We've spoken on the phone."

"Yes," Domini agreed, and felt her heart sink. "Were you looking for Mr. Wellby?"

"I was, but I can see I've missed the wretched man yet again. He's like the Scarlet Pimpernel, isn't he? We seek him here, we seek him there..."

Peering round at Jeff to make sure he couldn't overhear, Marguerite whispered, "You don't think he's trying to avoid me, do you?"

"I've no idea," Domini blinked. "He doesn't discuss his private life with me."

"Oh. Only he's definitely been a bit odd lately," she frowned. "Evasive."

"Perhaps he has something on his mind," Domini offered lamely.

"Yes, that's what worries me. I think it might be me—and how to off-load me gently. Best not tell him I was here," she whispered with a sort of belated discretion.

"No, I won't tell him."

"Well, don't *you* go and fall in love with him, will you?"

"No." Of course she wouldn't. No chance of that. "You should go before he comes back."

"Yes," Marguerite sighed. "Nice to have met you. Bye."

"Bye," Domini echoed as the other girl hurried out. Poor Marguerite. Why poor? she wondered. She'd seemed entirely philosophical about the whole thing. "She wasn't here," Domini told Jeff in an effort to distract herself.

"Who?"

With a wry smile, she got back to her report. Fall in love with him? No way. But why did she refuse to look up when he returned from lunch?

"What did Marguerite want?" he asked casually.

Was the place bugged? "How do you know she was here?"

"I saw her leave. So what did she want?"

"Nothing very much."

"Which is exactly what you told her, right?"

"Right," she sighed. "Flowers?"

"No. Don't you have to go to the bank, Jeff?"

"What?" Slightly startled, he blinked, then gave a resigned nod. "Right. Bank."

"Poor Jeff," Domini said. "Why on earth did you send him out?"

Settling himself on the corner of her desk, he gave her a long look. "Because I want to know about this compulsive interest you seem to have in my affairs."

"It's not compulsive!" she denied. "I haven't even mentioned them since I've been here!"

"So you haven't. Thought about them, though."

"No, I have not," she lied. "And if you would only explain to your *girlfriends* that I am not an information service..." And if he hadn't given a slow, mocking smile, she probably would have left it at that. "Although if she knows you as well as..."

"You do? You can only wonder why she bothers?" he finished for her. Reaching out, he drew her fiercely resisting body towards him. "This is why," he added softly before fastening his mouth on hers.

"Don't *do* that!" Domini shoved Jack away.

"So morally superior, aren't you?" he taunted.

"Thank God," she retorted. "And you're wearing lipstick!" There was something so very—disturbing about seeing a man with traces of your own lipstick on his mouth. Dragging a tissue out of the box on her desk, she thrust it at him. He proffered his chin.

"No?" he teased when she refused to wipe it away. "Spoil-sport." Taking the tissue, he did it himself. "Now, get your coat—we have a meeting to attend."

She opened her mouth to argue, and closed it firmly again. His behaviour wasn't even worth commenting on. "Where are we going?" she asked stiffly.

"Near Gatwick, and don't sulk."

"I am not su—"

"Just let it be a lesson to you, Miss Keane. If you don't want the consequences, keep that pretty little nose out of my private affairs."

"I would be more than happy to," she told him wrathfully, "if you didn't keep dragging them into the office! And let me tell you," she added indignantly, "that *you* can hardly be called consistent about the matter!"

"That's what makes me such a good business-man," he allowed blithely, "my ability to adapt to any given situation, business or otherwise. Well, come along. I want to look at this ware-house before dark. Ah, Jeff, what excellent tim-ing. Man the phone, will you? And ring Reg Prior to tell him I'm on my way."

What warehouse? And why was she needed?

"You drive," he told her. "I had wine at lunch."

Then why didn't he get a cab? Why drink wine when he knew he had to go out?

"Which way?"

"I will leave it entirely to you," he said.

Ignoring him, she drove towards Blackheath, then picked up the bypass that would take them to the M25. Following the signs for the airport, then his verbal directions along a country lane, she parked on a piece of waste ground.

"Tuck in behind the hoarding. I don't want someone scratching the car."

Who? she wondered blankly. There was no one around! And the warehouse rose less than majestically from a sea of rubbish.

He climbed from the car, giving her a mocking look, and began to pick his way towards the building. Neither of them was dressed for this sort of exercise, she thought irritably, both in formal suits, and she with the added disadvantage of high-heeled shoes!

"Certainly looks large enough. The freight company I partially own needs expansion," he explained casually as he slid the huge wooden door to one side.

How exciting. "Based in Gatwick, is it?" she asked.

"Mmm. Might as well have a look round while we're waiting for Reg." Taking her arm, he helped her over the metal lip, and they both stared into the empty cavern. There was a flight of rickety stairs to one side. "Seem strong enough," he murmured as he began to climb.

Watching him, and still feeling a desire to shove him off a high place, she followed him. The stairs led to a railed gallery that ran round three sides of the building, and they began to walk along it. The roof was made up of peaked skylights, wired for strength, which gave plenty of light. There were a few pieces of cardboard lying around, a piece of sacking, and very little else. "What exactly do you need the building for?"

"Storage?" he asked with mild sarcasm, but his heart wasn't in it, and he grinned. "War, is it?"

"No, I just don't like..." Breaking off, she frowned. "That sounded like..."

"The door," he finished. Swinging away, he called, "Reg? Reg!" as the door was slammed shut, followed by the sounds of a padlock being applied. "Hey!" he shouted, dashing down the stairs. He slammed his hand flat on the door. "Hey!" There was only the sound of a truck starting up. "Oh, bloody hell!"

"We're locked in?" she asked as she went down to join him.

"Yes, Miss Keane! Meaning Reg isn't coming, or he did, but didn't see the car, and decided *I* wasn't!"

"Well, you'd think he would have looked inside!"

"You would indeed. And the phone is in the car. Damn." Swinging to face her, he asked, "Is there anyone to worry if you're late home?"

She shook her head. "You?"

"Not really. Certainly no one concerned enough to tell anyone, like the police. But fear not, Miss Keane, I will look after you."

Yes, that was what worried her. Being locked in, she could cope with. Being locked in with a wickedly challenging Jack Wellby was another matter.

With a smile she wasn't sure she trusted, he continued, "And as I always prided myself on my ingenuity, now would seem like a good time to test it."

Starting with the wall to his left, he began sounding it with his hand as he walked. Domini watched him. She didn't think he would find any weak spots, or not any sufficiently weak to enable him to make a hole with his bare hands. And there wasn't anything else—no implements of any kind.

Glancing up at the skylights, she had another idea. Reclimbing the stairs, she walked to the front of the building. Could she hurl something through them?

"Take off your shoes," Jack said from so close behind her that she jumped.

"What? They're not heavy enough to break the glass."

"I wasn't intending to. Anyway, it's wired."

"Then why do you want my shoes?"

"I don't. I just don't want you standing on my shoulders with them on."

"Oh. You want me to look out of the skylight and try to attract attention?"

"Worth a try, don't you think?"

"Definitely." Well, it was; it was just the thought of standing on his shoulders that was rather alarming. Think of him as a brother, she told herself. Pretend it's Nick, or David. When he crouched, using the wall for balance, she climbed onto his back. As he straightened, she stepped carefully onto his shoulders. Hooking her fingers over the high window-ledge, she slowly raised herself and peered out. "I can see the road."

"Good," he commented drily.

"Unfortunately," she went on, "it's empty. Even if a car did go by I doubt they would look... Hey! There's one!" Letting go, she slammed both hands on the glass, tried frantically to attract attention, wobbled, and frantically grabbed the window-ledge.

"For God's sake!" Jack exploded. "Did he see you?"

"No," she said despondently.

"Then we'd best think of something else, otherwise one or other of us is liable to break their neck!"

Glancing down, seeing how near the railing was, how near to a disaster they might have been, she nodded.

Standing with their backs to the wall, they both stared round at their prison. "What about a sign? One of the lower windows has a rusty catch, which must mean it once opened. If we could make a sign, hang it out..."

"Help? We're locked in?" he mocked.

"Yes," she insisted. "It's worth a try, isn't it?"

"I suppose," he admitted. "It won't show up on cardboard or sacking, will it?"

"No." With a slightly malicious smile, she looked at his white shirt. So did he, and began to remove his jacket.

"Good job it's a mild winter."

When he'd removed his shirt and shrugged back into his jacket—with her managing *not* to look at a naked expanse of chest—she spread it out, and carefully printed in red lipstick, "HELP. WE'RE LOCKED IN!!!" And then underlined it with black eyeliner pencil. "Will that show up, do you think?"

Staring thoughtfully down at his ruined shirt, he took the pencil and carefully outlined each letter.

"That's better," she approved warmly.

"Thank you," he said drily. "OK, up you go again."

Carefully laying the shirt along the sill so that the message would be clearly displayed, she closed the window and latched it to hold the shirt in place, then frowned thoughtfully. "Do you think we should have weighted the bottom so that it hung flat?"

He sighed, "Yes," he agreed. "Sorry, my fault. I don't seem to be thinking straight—probably due to the proximity of long nylon-clad legs," he added under his breath. "But it's not windy out today. We'll just have to hope for the best. Come on, down you come."

"Will Jeff be expecting you back?" she asked.

"No. Now we just wait," he confirmed, heading down the stairs. "I could murder a pint," he murmured.

"Mmm," she agreed, "although I'd prefer a gin and tonic."

"Cheese and biscuits. Coffee."

"Strawberry ice-cream."

Sitting on the bottom step, he put his chin in his hands.

"So, how long do you think it will take?" she pleaded.

"Half an hour to see the sign. Half an hour to get help. Half an hour to find the owner. Hour and a half?"

"Should be free by half-past six."

"Or less—then I'll buy you a gin and tonic."

"I'll hold you to that."

"Of course, Reg might ring Jeff, and he'll tell him we're here . . ."

"And he'll come back. . . ."

Eyes widening, she broke off, and listened. "Car!" she yelled and rushing over to the door, she began hammering on it. Jack remained sitting on the stairs and watched her efforts with amusement.

When silence reigned once more, she gave him a reproving glance. "You might have helped."

"Why? If the sign had been seen, the natural reaction would be to stop, come over, bang on the door and call, 'Is anybody there?' Whereupon we would have leapt to our feet and shouted, 'Yes!' ''

"Oh, shut up," she grumbled. "Know it all, don't you?"

"I wish." With a sympathetic smile he asked, "Fed up?"

"Yes. Sorry." She looked up. "Be dark soon. You don't think we'll be here all night, do you?" she asked. "I don't like the dark."

"Shouldn't think so for a minute," he comforted. "Why don't you like the dark?"

"It makes me feel vulnerable. I got locked in the cellar once, when I was a little girl. I was in there for hours."

"Come and sit down."

Immediately wary, she returned to the stairs.

"Sit on this one," he patted the stair beside him.

"No," and gathering her coat under her, she sat two below him.

"Why so far away?" he asked.

"Because . . ." Because what?

"Come on," he encouraged. "I promise to behave."

With a wry smile, she reproved, "I don't think your idea of behaving and mine coincide somehow." So she stayed where she was—and he moved down to join her. When he put his arm round her, she tried to pull away.

"Stop worrying about it. Everything will be fine. Not been your day, has it?"

"No." Telling herself that she wasn't tense, that his closeness did not make her nervous, she tried to relax—and found it impossible.

"You smell nice."

"Thank you," she whispered warily.

"You feel nice."

"Thank you," she murmured, her throat dry.

"And I terrify the hell out of you, don't I?"

Snapping upright, she denied forcefully, "You do not!"

"Good." And he kissed her.

"Don't do that!" she snapped.

"Why?"

"Because I don't want you to!"

"But you're here. I'm here. We're both bored."

"I do not kiss people out of boredom!"

"You don't?" he teased. "All right, not out of boredom, but because you are wholly delightful and attractive—and it will pass the time very nicely."

"You promised to behave!" she said tartly.

"I am behaving. You should see me when I'm not," and, before she could comment, he leaned forward, teased her lips apart—and kissed her as she had never been kissed in all of her twenty-nine years.

When he eventually broke the kiss she stared at him, her eyes wide—shocked, almost.

"Not very experienced, Domini?" he asked gently.

"No." Not with men of his calibre, anyway. And yet when he drew her gently back she didn't resist but melted against him, allowed the kiss to deepen, kissed him back, almost as though she had been wanting to do so for a very long time.

The wood was cold beneath her skirt, hard against her back, the sharp ridge of the step digging into her spine, and she felt none of it, felt only warm and wanting, and special. Her hand slid to the opening in his jacket, touched the warm flesh of his chest; and then, as though that weren't enough, she slid both arms round to his strong back, hugged him to her.

His long fingers played with her lips, teased them apart, kissed them, moved her lower lip a fraction and kissed her again, his finger still in place. Delicately touching his fingertips inside her mouth, he parted his lips to cover them, and it was the most erotic thing that had ever happened to her.

Her eyes closed, she traced his ribs, his narrow waist, his chest, his neck, as he continued to play with her mouth like a musician. Such soft, gentle movements, so very arousing. But then the gentle rise and fall of his chest against her hands was arousing. One of his arms held her to him, his hand cupping her shoulder; the other, fingers spread, continued to tease her mouth, touch her cheeks, her eyelids, the lobe of her ear. So soft, barely discernible. Special. Like a dream.

And when he'd finished exploring her mouth, he moved to her neck, and she shivered, arched against him, acquiescent now. Her coat, jacket and the wide neck of her sweater were teased aside; the hollow formed by her shoulder was examined softly, licked; the upper swell of her breast was delicately traced, and she felt suffocated. Sweet pain lanced downwards, warmed her stomach, tightened it, fled to her groin, and she wanted to rip off her top, expose herself to his seeking mouth—and she couldn't believe she was allowing him such licence. And now his fingers were beneath her top, at her waist, creeping slowly upwards; a thumb brushed the underside of her breast and was withdrawn. His other hand released her shoulder, arched to touch her hair, behind her ear, and his mouth returned to hers, began all over again.

Sliding one hand upwards, she touched his face, cupped his cheek, slid her fingers into his thick hair, and he changed his grip, moved her, drew her head round to lay across his updrawn knees, stared at her until she reluctantly opened her eyes. And he didn't say a word, just watched her, trailed his fingers across her flushed cheeks.

It was growing swiftly dark now, and, feeling drugged and unreal, she stared up at him, obediently parted her mouth when a finger lightly probed, and bit it gently on the tip. With his other hand, he drew her fingers towards his own mouth, parted it, and the sight of her blood-red nail against his lower lip, against his tongue, sent fresh warmth coursing through her. He tasted each finger in turn, his eyes on hers, moved his own fingers against her lip, sought out her tongue, and she shivered, caught in the spell. And then he raised his knees yet further, hooked his heels up another step, brought her face closer—and something changed. She saw the knowledge of desire, the hunger in his shadowy eyes, and, teasing no longer, he parted her mouth with urgent demand, held her that much tighter, and, breathless, she tried to pull away.

"Jack..."

"That's the first time you've used my name," he murmured thickly.

"No..." Sounding strangled, she tried to push him away, fought to ignore the pervasive quality of the kiss. Knowing that it was a battle she would lose, wanted to lose, she shoved harder. His heels slipped off the steps and she went sprawling—just as someone hammered on the door.

Three

"Jack? You in there?"

His breathing ragged, Jack observed, "Someone else with perfect timing." Getting to his feet, he stepped over her and walked to the door. "Yes," he called. "I'm here."

Feeling like a discarded doll, embarrassed—no, mortified—that she had so lost control of herself, she got slowly to her feet. And she knew, didn't she, what Marguerite had known? Understood how it felt to be discarded. So let that be a lesson to you, Domini—don't take him seriously. Only it didn't feel, at the moment, as though that was going to be very easy.

As the heavy door was slid back she stared at the grinning idiot illuminated by powerful headlights, almost hating him for being late, for allowing what had happened to happen.

"You really like the warehouse, huh?" he asked.

"Yes, it's fine," Jack agreed with a total lack of interest. "Can we leave now?"

"We?" Peering past Jack, his grin widened. "Oh, my." Reg gave an approving whistle, and Domini gave him a look that would have made Medusa proud. He smiled shamefacedly, then apologised. "Sorry." Turning to Jack, he almost babbled. "It seems we all got the timing wrong. I rang the office to say I would be a bit late, Jeff said he would ring you in the car to tell you, and the idiot who owns the warehouse sent some stroppy individual to unlock, which he did, then he decided no one was coming, and locked up again. He stupidly didn't check if there was anyone inside first..."

"Not only stupid, but deaf," Jack put in flatly. Then, glancing at his watch, he added, "It's still fairly early, so if neither of you has any objection, I'd like to get a preliminary report thrashed out tonight."

Would it do them any good to have objections?

Without waiting for an answer, he continued, "Reg, you return the key, nose around discreetly at Blakely's, find out whether anyone else is interested, that sort of thing—and let me know. Tonight. Domini and I will go and draft the report.''

Would they? And who was Blakely? She would find out soon enough.

Still feeling dazed, she climbed behind the wheel. Presumably his alcohol level was still too high to drive. Her emotion level was probably too high to drive. Oh, God. ''To your house?'' she queried quietly.

''Yes.'' He sounded terse.

It wasn't far to his home, and they drove there in silence. Parking tidily, she switched off the engine just as a grey Metro swerved in. There was a blonde at the wheel.

''No need to look so sour, Miss Keane,'' Jack reproved testily. ''It's Sally, my sister-in-law.''

''Oh.''

''Yes, that about sums it up, doesn't it?'' he commented quietly as he climbed out.

She watched Jack greet his sister-in-law, who, to Domini's surprise, gave him a look of dislike.

''Another one?'' she sneered. ''Every time I see you it's a different woman. What happened to Marguerite?''

''History,'' he told her flatly. ''And this is not another woman—it's my secretary.''

"Oh, is that what you're calling them now?" With a derisive toss of her head, she walked inside.

He shrugged. "Take no notice. She disapproves of my lifestyle—and her manners leave a lot to be desired. Come on."

Sure. And since when had secretaries become unsexed? Since he had kissed one?

"Go on into the study," he ordered when they were inside. "I'll go and organise some food."

When he returned, he'd changed, dragged on a navy sweater over his suit trousers, and he gave her a searching glance as he came in carrying a tray with sandwiches and a pot of tea, setting it on the desk. "If you don't mind, I'd like to get down a file note, an *aide-mémoire*, impressions, options, and then, when I've received Reg's report, we can draft out a rent agreement."

"Yes, of course," she agreed.

"Then, if you could type it up on the computer in the corner, it would be a big help."

Nodding, she kept her eyes on her pad, and waited.

"And as for what happened . . ."

Her heart thudded. "I don't want to talk about it."

"We have to talk about it. If we don't it will fester away and ruin our working relationship. There was a momentary—attraction—"

Flinging her head up, she said, "I just told you I didn't want to talk about it! And I *certainly* don't want to hold a discussion on its merits or otherwise!"

"Oh, stop over-reacting!" he reproved crossly. "And, seeing as neither of us wants an emotional entanglement," he continued firmly, "I—"

"Then you shouldn't have done it!" she burst out.

"I know that, dammit!" he shouted. Raking his hand through his hair, he swung away, took a determined breath, and turned back to face her. "All right, I'm sorry," he apologised quietly. "It was my fault, but all I'm trying to say is it did happen, but we're both adults, both capable of backing off. So we'll deny the attraction, make sure it never happens again. Right?"

"Right," she agreed tightly. That easy, was it?

He perched on the edge of his desk, glanced at her rather broodingly, and then began to dictate. "*Aide-mémoire*. Today's date. Proposed storage facility."

When he had finished he said quietly, "I'll leave you to type it in peace. I have some calls to make. I'll do them in the lounge so that you won't be disturbed."

"Thank you." Disturbed? Who the hell was disturbed?

He left without further comment, and she moved across to the computer and turned it on. Why on earth hadn't she asked him to dictate it straight to the screen? It would have saved so much time. Pouring herself a cup of tea, and putting two sandwiches on a plate, she settled herself down to transcribe the notes.

She was vaguely aware of peripheral sounds—of the children, the sound of the phone ringing—and, her mind only half on what she was doing, she continued to worry about what had happened in the warehouse. Deny the attraction? Episode over? He'd been bored, and she'd just been there? The sudden ping of the fax machine made her jump, and she closed her eyes briefly in defeat. At this rate she'd be a nervous wreck in no time. She went to collect the pages that Reg had faxed through, then walked to the door and opened it. Diddy and Jack were outside, and clearly some drama was going on. Jack looked distracted, Diddy as though she was about to cry.

"Oh, I'm sorry," she apologised. "The fax from Reg."

"Mmm? Oh, thanks." Taking it, he returned his attention to Diddy. "I could probably get someone from the agency..."

"No, you can't do that. First their mother disappearing off to Scotland, then me... No. I can't go, and that's the end of it."

Jack turned to Domini and explained, "Diddy's sister has had a heart attack and she's in Intensive Care."

"Oh, Diddy," she exclaimed. "I'm so sorry. Of course you must go!"

"I can't!" she wailed. "What about the children?"

"What about them? Mr. Wellby's here..."

"Domini," he protested, "I have a business to run!"

Giving Jack a little glare, Domini turned back to his housekeeper. "Of course you must go," she assured her. "Your sister comes first."

With a worried glance at Jack, who was still hesitant, Diddy gave a wretched little sigh. "Tom..."

"Tom will want to be with you," Domini added.

"Domini!" Jack barked.

Ignoring him, she told Diddy, "Go on. Go and get packed." As soon as she was out of earshot, Domini spat, "Don't you dare make her feel guilty! It's her sister!"

"I know who it is, thank you!"

"Then go after her, tell her it's all right—not so damned grudgingly that she feels even more wretched!"

He narrowed his eyes, turned on his heel, and walked after his housekeeper. With a shaken sigh, Domini turned back into the study. He probably had an army of people he could call on... He was making difficulties where none existed. Still angry, disillusioned, she finished the typing, then pressed the print button.

"Finished?" he asked tersely from behind her.

"Yes," she said.

"Good, and you will no doubt be pleased to know," he added, "that Diddy and her husband will be away shortly!"

"I'm very pleased to hear it."

"So I assumed—and if you ever," he said almost savagely, "take me to task in front of anyone again, I'll..."

"What? Sack me?"

He shook his head. "No, Miss Keane, but as you were so generous with my time I will allow you the dubious pleasure of bathing the children and putting them to bed!"

"Very well," she said stiffly.

"It also means that you will need to stay."

"Stay? Here, do you mean? Forget it!"

"I wish I could. But, owing to your meddling, a great many hours will now be wasted—so I will arrange for a car to take you home. You can then pack some things and return."

"No. I am not staying here!"

Leaning closer, his hands flat on his desk, Jack insisted softly, "Yes, Miss Keane, you are. When you have put the children to bed, you will return here, and we will thrash out this lease, for however long it takes. That means I need my secretary to hand. Doesn't it?"

"It does," she agreed tightly. "What it does not mean is that I have to spend any of my nights in this house! I can commute—"

"No. You offered your services as babysitter..."

"Well, you surely didn't expect Diddy to stay when her sister was so ill? Even *you* can't be that selfish!"

"I am not that selfish! What I am is busy! And if I don't remain busy," he snapped, "then I won't be able to afford to employ staff, will I? Including a secretary, who I am beginning to think is vastly overpaid! So you will put your emotions to one side . . . and let me get a car to take you home . . ."

"I will stay tonight until the draft is done, I will then go home—and return at eight in the morning."

"For a few days. Until Diddy or Sally gets back."

The journey back at that time of evening took just over an hour. Domini set the alarm for six, and fell asleep the moment her head touched the pillow.

It felt like only seconds later that the alarm woke her, and one eye on the time, she breakfasted and then quickly packed, defiantly adding a pair of jeans. If she was to go clambering around warehouses and deal with the children she wanted to be suitably dressed. But no way would she go clambering alone with Jack Wellby!

Taking her case out to the car, she glanced at the house to make sure it was all secure, and headed for Surrey. She pulled into Jack's driveway at exactly five minutes to eight—to yet more drama.

"Angus can't find one of his shoes," Jack informed her irritably as he opened the door.

Barely looking at him, she dumped her bag, eyed the angelic-looking Angus, and prompted softly, "Shoe?"

"Don't know," he beamed.

Wretch. "Then you will have to go to school without it, won't you?"

He screwed up his face, gave her a very adult, calculating look, decided she probably *would* send him to school with only one shoe, beamed, and scampered back upstairs. There was the sound of rummaging, and two minutes later he returned, with the shoe.

Smiling warmly down at him, her eyes full of laughter, she approved, "Good boy," then returned her attention to her boss, and, still barely making eye contact, she asked briskly, "Lunch boxes? Or do they take money?"

"How should I know?"

"By asking?" she returned sweetly. "Where's Amelia?"

"In the kitchen," and turning on his heel, he stalked off to the back of the house.

Holding out a hand for Angus, she followed. "Hello, again. Had breakfast?"

"Yes, thank you. Did Angus find his shoe?"

"He did. Now, do you take lunch boxes or money?"

"Lunch boxes. I already did them."

"Good girl."

Still ignoring Jack, who was standing, arms folded, by the table, she asked Amelia, "Do you know which room I will be using?"

She glanced at her uncle, then Domini. "Shall I show you?"

"Yes, please."

She only had time to dump her case and give the room a quick inspection. Had other women slept here? His other women? It was blue and gold, a beautiful room, feminine without being prissy. She ushered Amelia back downstairs, collected Angus and asked Jack, "You wish me to take them to school?"

"I do."

She had a brief word with the teachers, explaining who she was, that she would be collecting both Angus and Amelia, and returned to the house. Jack was in the study at the computer, too impatient to wait for her return. His typing consisted of the hunt-and-peck variety, and there was a look of frustration on his face.

"You'd like me to do that?" she asked in a very businesslike manner.

"Yes. I'll go and shower and change."

When he returned, dressed now in a dark grey suit, dark red tie and highly polished black shoes, she was scrolling through the report to check for spelling errors, grammar.

Using the same cool tone, he asked, "Finished?"

"Yes, just checking it." And as the familiar task absorbed her the tension slowly eased, until he came to lean on the back of her chair and peer at the screen.

"Change that," he suddenly ordered. "Not 'should,' 'will.'"

Ignoring his closeness as best she could, she altered the word.

"Right, that's fine. Print it out, will you? Then fax it to my lawyers for their input."

"Very well."

"Emphasise that we need it back by one at the latest. We're meeting Blakely at two... Damn," he muttered as the phone shrilled, "it's just one damned interruption after another." Reaching out, he snatched it up with an impatient gesture.

"Yes? What? Oh, for God's sake! All right," he resumed into the receiver, "give me a couple of hours and ring me if anything changes." He replaced the phone. "I'm needed in Poole, at one of my businesses—some dispute with the work-force." His heavy frown still in place, he added, "You'll have to attend the meeting with Blakely on your own. Reg will go with you. Stick to the agreement I've drafted. The only leeway I'll allow is on termination."

The meeting went very well. She got agreement on all the points Jack wanted, which was a marvellous booster of confidence. It was the little "friendly" gathering afterwards that caused her the problems. Their idea of "friendly" was to bombard her with lecherous suggestions, press unwanted drinks into her hand—which she refused because she had to drive—and try to pump her about her boss, her private life—even her sexual preferences!

Pleading an urgent appointment, she gave them all a brittle smile, made sure she had signed the agreement, and fled, to drive to the school.

Angus was the first out—why was she surprised? Amelia, fifteen minutes later, was the last. "What happens now?" Domini asked.

"We're allowed to watch television for a bit, then we have our tea."

Delivering them back to the house, surprised to see Jack's car in the drive, she ushered them inside, turned on the television, and walked along to the study.

"Hi," he smiled. "How did the meeting go?"

"Fine. You were quick."

"Mmm. Helicopter," he explained.

"Oh." Helicopter? She handed him the agreement. He glanced through it, whistled, smiled again. "Well done."

"Thank you," she approved somewhat tartly.

He raised his eyebrows in query. "Something wrong?"

"No," she denied. She decided to try for some humour. "What should be wrong? Your assumption that I might like to be pawed around by a lot of lecherous men who at barely midday seemed determined to consume vast quantities of liquor?"

"Oh, dear."

"Yes. And," she added, "I would have been enormously grateful for some sort of warning beforehand of what I was expected to cope with."

"And couldn't you?" he queried. "Cope?"

"Yes. And did."

"Of course, because I would never have sent you if I'd thought anything else. And," he added in deliberate warning, "I would never have employed you at all if I hadn't thought you could cope with *any* given situation."

She was stung into retorting, "Including the warehouse?"

His eyes narrowing, he nodded. "Yes." Then asked, "Children all right?"

"Yes. They're watching television—and then it will be their teatime."

Leaning back in his chair, he linked his hands behind his neck, and a little flame of devilment lit his eyes. "And who, Miss Keane, is cooking the said tea?"

"You."

He grinned. "Certainly—if you will kindly type up the report I have left on your desk." His smile mocking, he got to his feet and strolled out, then poked his head back in. "And next time I send you to a meeting, do try, Miss Keane, to stick to essentials. I do not necessarily want a character analysis on the —er—clients."

Jack came in just as she'd finished printing out the report, and she silently handed it to him. "I promised to tuck Amelia in, so while you read that I'll go and do it."

With an absent nod, he sat in his chair, put his feet up on the desk, and began to read through it.

The rest of the evening was spent dealing with correspondence, and when that was finished he picked up the pile of faxes that Jeff had sent through. "You go on up to bed," he said quietly. "I shan't need you again tonight. And—Domini? Thank you."

For what? Being a good girl? No, that wasn't fair. Grateful to be able to escape, she went out and up to her room. She had a long soak in the bath, and then went to bed. But not to sleep. Or not for a long time.

As soon as she returned from the school run next morning, it was back to being busy.

"Ah, there you are," Jack exclaimed as though he'd had no idea where she might have gone. "Get me on a flight to New York, will you?"

"New York?"

"Yes, Miss Keane, New York." He began to prowl around the small study. "I shall need you to take the signed lease over to Blakely—oh, and Amelia has a clinic appointment. That reminds me—Diddy rang. Her sister's out of danger, so send her some flowers, will you? Address on the pad by the phone. New York?" he prompted. "Today."

She reached for the phone. "First-class?"

"Of course. And why haven't those figures come through from Jeff?"

"How would I know? I've been on the school run, remember?"

He just looked at her. "Don't be lippy, Miss Keane—secretaries can so easily be replaced."

"So can bosses."

"And is that what you want to do?" he asked quietly.

Never to see him again? Never to have this buzz of working for him? "No," she admitted.

"Right. Good," he muttered. "What flight am I on?"

"I'm still waiting to speak to the travel agen... Hello? Yes, please, Gatwick if possible. Yes, hold on ... There's a flight in three hours," she told him. "Will that give you time to pack a bag?"

"Three hours is fine, and I don't need to pack a bag. Confirm it, will you? And then get me a cab." While she did so, he gathered up his papers, stuffed them into his briefcase, and collected his passport from the safe. "Tell Jeff to keep an eye on that Manton project, will you? Let me know if there's any change."

"Let you know where?" she asked drily.

"Mmm? Oh." With a rather distracted grin, he quickly scribbled two telephone numbers on a piece of paper. "The first is my New York apartment, the second is Tercar International, where I'll be during office hours."

"Fine, thank you. The cab is on its way."

"Good. I'll be gone about a week, maybe less, and I think when I get back that we need to have a good talk—oh, damn, that sounds like the cab now. I'll see you later." He hurried out, and she heard the front door close, heard the cab pull away. Talk?

Four

Diddy returned the next morning, and Domini thankfully handed the household reins back, returned home, and resolved yet again to be sensible. And her little house felt empty. It never had before. Trying to persuade herself that it was because she'd been living in a family environment—that it had nothing to do with Jack—and failing, she decided to decorate her bedroom to take her mind off it, off him. And if she couldn't? Then she must leave him. Forget him— which wouldn't be easy. There were always vivid reminders. Like Saturday's evening paper, which had a picture of Jack with a gorgeous redhead on his arm.

What on earth was he doing on the social page? Or in the paper at all? He was still in the States. Frowning, she read the caption.

Whether it be New York or Newington, the lovelies keep coming. And who is this one? Jack Wellby declined to comment. But she is, of course, the delightful Lady Annabel Halford. Did she follow him abroad hoping to snare the notoriously fickle Jack? We cannot say.

With a snort of derision, she tossed the paper aside—then rescued it, to stare again at the picture of her laughing boss. And wasn't that a minor member of the royal family in the background? Moved in rather exalted circles, didn't he?

Crumpling the paper, she went to get ready for bed. But instead of talking herself round as she usually managed to do, she settled further and further into depression. She got undressed and climbed into bed—well, on to the mattress that was downstairs because she couldn't stand the smell of paint in her bedroom—and then couldn't get to sleep. What if she hadn't been so determined not to be attracted to him? Would he have wanted further intimacies? No, because he had made it very clear that he didn't. And nor did she. Not with him.

Tossing and turning, she finally drifted off, only to be woken by the strident ringing of the doorbell.

Oh, now what? Probably kids mucking about. At two o'clock in the morning? Listening intently, she jumped when it rang again. An emergency? Her mother?

She peered through the front curtains. There was no police car outside, and she couldn't quite see the front door from this angle. When the bell rang again, she pulled on her dressing-gown and with the chain on the door, she cautiously opened it.

"What on earth are you doing here?" she demanded.

"Freezing," Jack said. "Come on, Domini, let me in."

I don't want to let you in. But she unhooked the chain and reluctantly held the door wide. "It's two a.m.!"

"Is it? Sorry, were you asleep?"

"Of course I was asleep."

"Oh, sorry, the bloody cab broke down. Driver couldn't extract anything intelligible from his squawk box and I couldn't find a blasted phone box that took money. Did you know they're all phone cards now?" he demanded.

"Yes."

Domini followed him into the lounge. He was in evening dress, the tie undone. He looked dishevelled, roguishly attractive, had probably been with a woman . . . She didn't know what to say to him and so took refuge in anger. "That still doesn't explain what you're doing here."

"What? Oh, I'd been to some charity do. Some idiot spiked the punch." He gave her a devastating smile. "You're looking very fetching," he added softly, pulling her gently towards him and looking down into her troubled face. "It's not going to go away, is it?" he asked. "This thing that's between us. It's like a spectre at the feast." He continued quietly, "When I first met you, I thought you were a tough little lady who knew all the answers, only you aren't, are you?"

"No," she whispered.

"And that makes it damnably hard, because I want to make love to you—very badly."

She felt a sick, spiralling feeling in her stomach, an excitement that she forcibly banished.

"Don't look so worried," he teased. "I've never used force in my life, and don't intend to start now. And I haven't just come from the arms of another woman," he added, as though mind-reading had just been added to his list of talents. "I've been celibate for weeks."

Had he? Because of her? Ah, no, and to believe him, let down this so very fragile barrier... Looking down, forcibly denying the attraction, she moved away, and with a picture of the lovely Lady Annabel still in her mind she asked, "When did you get back?"

"This afternoon."

"And you've had no sleep?"

"No," he replied wryly, "which is why I'm not at my best."

"How far have you walked?"

"From the church."

"Good job you remembered my address, then."

"Isn't it?" he asked blandly. "I'd previously looked it up on the A to Z for future reference. Why is there a mattress on the floor? Squatters?"

"No, I'm decorating my bedroom."

"Oh." He smiled, moved closer, and asked softly, "Do I owe you an apology?"

"No," she said, yearning for one. "I'll make you some coffee." And, without waiting for an answer, she went into the tiny kitchen, stiffening when he followed her.

"Anything happen while I was away?"

"No. All quiet." Go away, she silently pleaded, and when he did so with no prompting she leaned against the sink. Oh, God. Please don't let him mention making love any more.

Taking a deep, calming breath, she stared at the coffee-pot. And he'd said she looked fetching. In stripy silk pyjamas? She quickly made the coffee and took it through to the lounge. Jack was perched on the sofa absently glancing through one of her books, and if she sat beside him he would be too close. Handing him his coffee with a hand that shook, she began to straighten things that didn't need straightening.

Looking up at her under his lashes, he grinned and put the book to one side, sipping the hot liquid.

"What are you going to do now?"

With a shrug, he mused, "Get another cab, I suppose." He looked bewildered—jet lag, she assumed vaguely.

"I'll call you a cab," she said.

"Why are you in such an all-fired hurry to get rid of me? Expecting a lover?"

"No. Have you finished that coffee?"

"No."

Not wanting to make an issue of it, she did her best to keep calm—and it was all so silly. Why did Jack Wellby make her feel so nervous? Threatened? Aching?

"I did a lot of thinking when I was away," he went on, "about you, and how you had made me feel."

"I don't want to listen to this," she denied agitatedly. "People say all sorts of things when they've been drinking, when they're jet lagged..."

"And you think I don't know what I'm saying? And can you stand there and say, hand on heart, that I don't affect you?"

"No," she admitted, "but that doesn't mean I want anything further."

"Or won't allow yourself to want?"

"I just don't want to be hurt! And I would be if I allowed myself to be—attracted. I need something more than a casual liaison. Oh, this is a stupid conversation! I want to go to bed—and I want you to go. I'm going to ring for a cab."

"And what an absolute waste. Never to have a lover..."

"I did not say I had never had a lover," she retorted. "Only that I wasn't expecting one..."

"And that you didn't want me as one."

"Yes." He didn't sound even marginally interested.

"Was Lady Annabel there tonight?" she asked tartly.

"Who the hell is Lady Annabel?"

With a hollow laugh, she shook her head. "No one."

"Then why mention her?" he queried sleepily.

"I'll get your cab," she repeated. "Jack? Jack!" she said more loudly. But he was asleep. "Oh, you wretch!" Bending down, she removed his shoes, lifted his legs on to the sofa, decided she'd better remove his jacket, tugged gently on one sleeve—and he rolled on to the floor.

"Oh, for God's sake! Jack! You can't possibly be asleep after falling off the settee—and don't do that! Jack!"

His eyes still closed, he smiled, held her more tightly, and rolled with her on to the mattress. "That's better," he said. Easing out of his jacket, and still hanging onto her arm, he snuggled against her, dragging the duvet over them both, and mumbled, "I have to be up early."

The light was still on, and she could see him clearly. He looked younger in sleep, and she knew she shouldn't have done it, but she was tired, confused, and perhaps she just wanted to try to clarify her feelings. Clarify? Domini, you're in love with him, want to be held, loved, kissed. That incident in the warehouse had not been a fluke... And his mouth was very close, his body closer, and there was such a need inside her, so much love that she was afraid to give, that she pressed her mouth softly to his. And half asleep, he responded, then sleepily opened his eyes.

"Why are we in bed together?" he asked lazily.

"You fell off the settee."

"And then you kissed me."

"Proximity," she said promptly. "You're an attractive man. I was temp—testing," she hastily substituted.

"Mmm. So, it's either go home, go to sleep, or make love. It would be nice," Jack persuaded softly.

Oh, yes, it would be that—but if she couldn't get a kiss out of her mind, what about his love-making? She wouldn't. "No," she denied firmly.

"Unprofessional?" he mocked. "Or cowardly?"

"The former." And because she had to know, Domini asked, "What went wrong between you and Marguerite?"

With an exasperated sigh, he opened one eye. "She was beginning to bore me," he said. "She started to make wifely noises, but you aren't going to do that, are you? You aren't even going to make mistressy noises, so go to sleep. And since you are the best damned secretary I ever had, it's probably just as well," he mumbled before he went back to sleep.

Angrily twitching the cover aside, she scrambled free, yanked it back over him, and went to get a spare blanket. Wrapping it warmly round herself, she went to huddle on the sofa.

I don't like you, Jack Wellby, she told him silently. Then with an anguished little cry, she stared at him, his strong face, softer now, gentle... Blinking back tears, she extinguished the lamp and wished she could extinguish her feelings as easily. She didn't remember drifting into sleep, only the violent awakening....

"Domini!" Jack shouted. "It's nearly ten o'clock! I have to be in Surrey by twelve! Move, woman!"

"Don't 'woman' me," she complained, then asked, "Why by twelve?"

"Never mind why. Where's your bathroom?"

"Upstairs." Only she was talking to herself.

There was mist on the motorway—not enough to slow them dramatically, but enough to put Jack in a foul mood. They didn't talk—he very pointedly, she because she was hurting too badly. What could you say to a man who, just because you'd refused to sleep with him, was being disagreeable? What did you say to a man you loved, who didn't love you back? She was very thankful to finally reach his house. As she turned into his drive, intending to drop him and drive quickly away, she found her way blocked by a Land Rover and a smaller car. "Looks as if you have visitors," she said.

"Yes. Thank you for the lift," he murmured.

Before he could get out, an elderly, tweed-clad woman hurried towards them, beaming. "There!" she exclaimed. "I knew you wouldn't be late! And you've brought another helper! Wonderful."

"Elizabeth," Jack began, "I—"

"And I saw you all over the paper yesterday," she rushed on. "Kept quiet about the lovely Lady Annabel, didn't you?"

"Oh, God," he said wearily.

And she thrust the paper at him.

He glanced at it. "Yes, Lady Annabel. Whom I did not know. She saw the photographer, decided she wanted her picture taken, and grabbed my arm.''

"Oh," Elizabeth exclaimed, mentally echoed by Domini.

"Yes. Sorry to disappoint you," he said, "but I have not yet linked myself to the aristocracy." Levering himself upright again, he subsided when his housekeeper hurried out.

"There you are! I was beginning to get worried!" She smiled at Domini. "Hello, Miss Keane. Come to help?''

"No she hasn't," Jack said. "She gave me a lift home.''

"But now that she's here . . ." Diddy began.

"No, she has to get back. Don't you, Miss Keane?" Then, leaning closer, he taunted, "And you should be careful whom you judge, lest others judge you in return." Getting out, he strolled towards the house.

"Oh, dear," Diddy exclaimed. "In one of his moods, is he? Well, no need to take any notice," she assured Domini. "Do you really have to get back? Because we could use your help."

"Will you?" Elizabeth said.

"Yes, but will I what?''

"You don't know?''

"No.''

"Well, you'd have thought he'd have let his secretary know," Diddy murmured.

"On the weekend nearest to Valentine's Day there's always a charity ball on the Saturday to raise money for children with special needs—he had to go yesterday without getting any sleep— and on the Sunday we hold a party for them. Jack arranges it, and Elizabeth here is in charge of transport. The children have varying disabilities—muscular dystrophy, cerebral palsy, Down's syndrome... And their school only has one minibus..."

"Which isn't enough," Elizabeth put in, "so I blackmail, plead, beg anyone with a car to help. So will you?"

"Help transport them?" But Jack didn't want her to, did he? Only how could she refuse? She couldn't—and there was also the desire to see Jack in a role she would never have imagined him in. Realising that the two women were still waiting for an answer, she gave a reluctant nod.

The revving of an engine diverted Domini's attention, and she turned to watch Diddy's husband Tom drive the vintage Bentley out of the garage. He left the engine running, and hurried across to the Land Rover. Two minutes later Jack, dressed now in jeans and a sweatshirt, strode across to his car and climbed in. Domini followed the convoy to the school and they were soon all on their way to the hotel.

"Still here, Miss Keane?" Jack derided as he walked past, pushing a wheelchair.

"Yes—Jack, look, I'm sorry. I didn't know—"

"Nor would you now if Elizabeth could just keep her mouth shut."

"Are you staying?" Diddy asked her, helping the last child out of Domini's car.

"No," she replied, because Jack didn't want her here, didn't want her anywhere near his pet project. "I promised to go and see my brother— at the university. But I will come back at—six o'clock?" Diddy nodded. "Have a lovely party."

Climbing quickly behind the wheel, she reversed out and then had to stop for a minute. There was a great big lump in her throat, not only because of the children, but because she felt choked and rejected. She *wanted* to be a part of it, only Jack had made it very clear that it wasn't what he wanted.

Not knowing where to go with six hours to kill, she drove towards the university. Might as well make fiction fact—if she could find her brother, that was.

She did find him, and even took him out to lunch, where he ate hungrily and she only picked; then she pretended she yearned to see the cathedral, and that took another hour. Later, she forced herself to eat a sandwich and have a cup of tea at a service-station restaurant, then drove back to the hotel.

There was still half an hour to go, so she went inside and peeked into the ballroom.

There were paper hats, streamers, balloons and smiling waiters and waitresses. A game was in progress, and Jack was kneeling on the floor, one little boy on his back, a little girl between his outstretched arms, trying to blow a balloon along the floor in a straight line, but he was laughing so much that it went every which way. He looked so different, as though he adored the children, and they quite obviously adored him, and she wondered again why on earth he didn't want to marry, have children of his own.

"Not going in, miss?"

Swinging round, she stared blankly at the man behind her. "No," she said. "I'll wait out here until they're finished."

"I can get you a cup of tea if you'd like?"

"Thank you, that would be nice."

"Regular card, isn't he?" he added, nodding at Jack. "Comes every year?"

"Yes," she agreed lamely, not knowing if it was true.

"Pays for it out of his own pocket, too?"

"Yes." She didn't know *that*, either.

"Philandering Jack. Isn't that what they call him?"

Alerted by his curiosity, she said frostily, "I have no idea."

"Sorry," he said, "didn't mean to offend. You a friend of his?"

"His secretary. Tea?" she prompted.

"Oh, right." With a smile, he hurried away, and didn't come back—but, before she could investigate, the doors opened and the children began to come out, all laughing and happy. She gave Jack a brief smile.

He gave her one back. And then he walked on.

After a sleepless night, she was late in. Jeff gave her an odd glance, and Jack didn't come in until lunchtime, which meant she spent her morning on edge. But why the look of fury? Why did he stride over to her desk—and wait?

"Is something the matter?"

"Yes, Miss Keane. Jeff, go to the bank."

Jeff hastily went.

"Yesterday," he began, "you wondered why I had not told you about the special needs children."

"Yes," she agreed warily.

"Then I will tell you. I do not do this in order to have people say, 'Oh, he must be a nice person if he does that,'" he derided savagely. "I do it because I want to, and hope, in its small way, that it is of help! And because I enjoy it! I do *not*, Miss Keane, do it in order to gain publicity! The ball on the Saturday is public, to raise funds! The party on the Sunday is a private thing! Or was!" He slapped the midday paper on the desk. "Now, thanks to you, it is no longer!"

Glancing down, she saw a blurred picture of herself beside her car, and of Jack pushing the wheelchair with little Tom King in it. A zoom lens, probably, and then she began to read. "Oh, it's not true," she exclaimed. "I didn't—"

"Didn't tell a reporter that I was Philandering Jack? That I do it each year? Pay for it out of my own pocket? That I'm having an affair," he sneered, "with my secretary?"

"No! I didn't," she insisted. "I don't even *know* any reporters. I..." Breaking off, she gasped, "The waiter... at least I thought he was a waiter—at the hotel, just before you all came out... He said... And I said yes. Oh, God."

"I once asked for your loyalty and discretion..."

"You've had it..."

"Yes," he agreed bitterly. "Haven't I just! I paid you to put my interests first..."

Staring at him, she swallowed hard. "And if I can't?" she managed. "Is that what you're saying?"

"Yes!" he agreed fiercely.

"I see."

"Good." Turning away, he slammed out.

Blinking rapidly to clear her vision, she reached out a shaking hand to switch off the computer. Not doing something deliberately didn't make it better.

Emptying her desk, she locked the filing cabinets, put the keys on Jack's desk, and left. There was a tight pain in her chest, an ache, and she didn't think she had ever felt so desolate in her entire life.

Five

When she woke next morning, heavy-eyed, Domini saw it was raining, and dull depression settled on her like a cloud. Then the television repair man arrived, abominably cheerful. Had she called him? Yes, she supposed she must have done, *again*.

Retreating to the kitchen, trying to summon up some interest in making breakfast, she heard him speak to someone outside. Now what?

"Shouldn't leave that there, mate. Madam's very particular about things left on her doorstep."

Just because she'd told him not to leave his tatty workbag on her clean step for anyone to fall over, she thought indignantly. Shoving open the kitchen door, she went to see who he was upsetting. Jack was standing on her doorstep, drip-

ping umbrella in hand. He didn't look entirely—
friendly.

He saw her, raised his eyebrows in query, and
waited.

And she didn't know what to do. She wanted
to rush back into the kitchen, pretend he wasn't
there—only she couldn't do that, could she? And
the repair man was still there, waiting, a look of
avid curiosity on his face. Giving him a frosty
look, she asked pointedly, "Have you finished?"

"Who, me? No, luv."

"Then would you kindly get on with it?"

"Sure." With a grin that looked more malicious than humourous, he edged past her and
returned to the dismembered television set.

"Can I come in?" Jack asked with some irri-
tation. "Or are we to conduct a conversation on
the doorstep that no one is allowed to dirty?"

Her mouth tight, she snatched his umbrella,
shook it briskly, and put it into the vase by the
front door. "I don't want you here."

"No, not being entirely insensitive to atmo-
sphere, I can see that." He stepped inside and
closed the door.

"Domini—"

"Go away."

"No, and it isn't what you want, not really..."

"Yes, it is." She swallowed hard. "Please, Jack..."

The door suddenly opened. "'Scuse me, miss, sir," the repair man said evilly. "Need to get something from the van."

Giving the man a look of dislike, Jack took her arm and edged her out of the way. "Who the hell *is* that?"

"Television repair man."

"Well, can't you tell him to come back later?"

"No, if I do that he won't come back at all."

With a wry smile, he propelled her towards the kitchen and firmly closed the door against any further intrusions. Leaning back against it, he asked quietly, "Will you answer one question?"

"What?" she asked warily.

"If I weren't the way you thought I was... what would have happened between us?"

Her eyes wide, she whispered, "I don't know."

"Don't you?" Watching her, he continued. "I thought at first that it would be a glorious game. You were twenty-nine, old enough to be experienced..."

"Only I wasn't—"

"I know," he agreed gently. "And you made it so very clear that I was not to—importune, and that intrigued me."

"I wasn't trying to intrigue you," she denied.

"I know, and that brought about the very thing you were trying so desperately to avoid. Oh, Domini," he sighed. "You were efficient, intuitive, trustworthy..."

"Until I spoke to that reporter." She added in a quiet little voice, "I'm so sorry about that..."

"It doesn't matter. Really. I was angry because I thought you had done it deliberately, to get back at me. But you aren't malicious, and no matter how much you might dislike me and all I stand for—"

"I don't dislike you," she murmured, her throat dry. And, dear God, she didn't. She wished she could.

"No? You have every reason to. I haven't behaved very well of late, have I? And that was partly why I was angry, at myself, at you, and because of injured pride. When you opened the door to me that night, looking soft, vulnerable, sweet and so very worried—I just wanted to love you. I..." With a little grunt of exasperation as the door behind him jarred against his heels, he wrenched it open and glared at the repair man. "What the hell are you doing?"

"Trying to get in! I need to speak with the missus!"

"Well, speak to her some other time! She's busy!"

"Ain't up to you..."

"No?" he asked coldly. With one long finger, he prodded the man backwards, followed him into the lounge, gathered up his tools, handed them to him, and escorted him to the front door, which he then slammed shut. He smiled at Domini and ushered her into the lounge. "I'll get someone in to repair the TV later."

"Yes," she said blankly.

With a wide, warm smile, he gathered her gently into his arms. "My darling, you look shell-shocked."

"Yes, that's how I feel. I didn't expect to see you again—and now I can't seem to..." Staring up at him, she tried to convince herself that this was real, that he seemed to be saying...

"I want you to be my wi... Domini, you're shaking. It's not that bad, is it?"

"No," she denied. "What did you say?"

"That I want you to be my wife."

"But you don't want a wife," she said stupidly.

"Didn't," he corrected, and bending his head, he parted her mouth slowly, oh, so slowly, and she sagged bonelessly against him. Oh, dear God. His wife? To have and to hold from this day forward... Still shaking, still not understanding how it had come about, not even caring, she kissed him back. Questions, answers could all come later.

"Pity you moved the mattress," he breathed, his beautiful voice thick, husky.

"It's upstairs," she murmured, almost afraid to move her mouth from his—a problem he solved by scooping her up and edging through the door with her and up the stairs. Laying her on the bed, he knelt to join her.

"Pick up where we left off?" he encouraged throatily.

With a little shiver of anticipation, remembering oh, so vividly her feelings in the warehouse, she nodded.

"I waited around all day, when I found you gone from the office." His long fingers disposed of the front fastenings of her shirt and he bent to trail his mouth across the swell of each full breast, playing havoc with her senses.

"Sacked from the office," she corrected throatily as her own hands began to explore the warmth and hardness of his body and pushed buttons through buttonholes. "Don't we have too many clothes on?"

"No, I want to undress you myself, and I didn't sack you.... Oh, God, don't do that..."

"Why not?"

"Because..." With a long shudder, he dragged in a deep breath, touching a finger to the zip of her jeans, applying downward pressure.

Watching him, loving him, not caring what tomorrow might bring, she raised her hips so that he could ease the denim free, and asked huskily, "What happens next?"

"This." He slowly, enjoyably removed the rest of her clothing, then, leaning forward, he bit ever so softly on her lower lip. "And this..." Cradling her warm, naked body in his arms, he began sending the most amazing sensations to every message-receiving nerve in her entire frame. There was the hazy thought that she should be doing something back, but it was lost in the desire to merge with him wholly, completely, to melt into his embrace.

There was a slow inevitability about it all, a hypnosis, a desire never to wake, to remain suspended in beautiful warmth. His mouth was unbelievably practised, and she would never have believed that knuckles could be such an instrument of pleasure, that a judiciously placed finger could draw forth her soul.

"I just love all these little noises you're making," he observed wickedly.

Lifting weighted lids, she stared into his eyes. She hadn't even been aware of making any noises. "And I just love those little things you keep doing to me."

His chuckle was soft, rich, warm as cream. "And you feel boneless, weightless, malleable..."

"Yes," she agreed, "but oh!" she exclaimed. "Is that allowed?"

"Certainly, and this, and this, and definitely this."

"Oh, yes, definitely that," she agreed with a long shudder.

Getting rid of the rest of his clothes was easy. He just got up, took them off, smiled warmly, and she saw that he was lean, strong, fit, very, very aroused, and probably the most exciting lover in the world.

Anticipation and a desperate need of fulfillment momentarily tensed her muscles, until he pulled her warm body to his, and she dragged in a shaky breath, released it, tried to relax.

He didn't use her; he used himself for her pleasure, and ultimately his own, and she felt oh, so special, oh, so loved. There had sometimes been the vague feeling in the past that she might have been missing something; now she knew that she had. She knew now what writers and poets eulogised about.

When it was possible to think again, she opened her eyes, stared at him, and gave him a funny little smile.

"Suddenly shy?" he asked gently. "Please don't be. You have a beautiful body, and," he teased, "you're definitely earthy and very, very sensuous."

"I never have been before."

"No? Then that makes me an incredibly lucky man."

"Mmm," she agreed with a little smile of her own. "No longer want to back off?"

"No, nor have I for some time. And the two *A*s will adore to have you as their aunty. You will be their aunty, won't you?"

"If you say the one thing you haven't said."

Leaning up on one elbow, staring down at her, he asked teasingly, "What? Sorry?"

"No."

"Please?"

"No."

"Domini! What?" he laughed. "I love you! I—"

"That's it."

She could see him mentally backtracking—then he grinned. "I did tell you!"

"No, you didn't."

"Then I'll tell you now. I love you, very much. More than very much. Hopelessly, helplessly, devotedly—um—"

"Kiss me!" she interrupted urgently.

He broke off, touched his mouth to hers, moved to her ear, whispered something.

"Jack!" she exclaimed in shock.

"What?" he asked innocently.

"That's indecent!"

"Is it? Oh, I never knew that. Learn something every day, don't you? Don't want me to do it, then?"

"I didn't say that," she said, "but not yet. I want to ask you something."

"Oh—oh," he exclaimed. "OK. Yes, I'm probably guilty of all you're going to accuse me of. No, my lifestyle is not as—ardent as the papers make out. It wouldn't be, would it? I'd never have the time to run a business! And I'm not *really* a womaniser, just have a healthy appetite—''

"Jack," she broke in, "appetite I know about. What I wanted to know was—why did you never want to get married?''

"I just never met anyone I wanted to marry! And it seemed safer to make the position clear... All my life, people have wanted things from me—and you never did. That was the beginning, I think. And then, in the warehouse, no matter how I tried to explain it away, I had never—*never*,'' he emphasised, "felt that extra warmth, that *feeling* when you kissed me back— as I want you to kiss me back now," he urged thickly. "And I think we've done enough talking.''

"Do you?" she asked huskily. "And, apart from that, what else would you like me to do?''

Curling himself warmly against her, fitting her generous curves to his lithe, masculine frame, he whispered, "Invent."